KYNDAL'S DREAM
adventure:
BECOMING A LEPRECHAUN

WRITTEN BY KYNDAL PARKER

ILLUSTRATED BY HH-PAX

XULON PRESS

Xulon Press
2301 Lucien Way #415
Maitland, FL 32751
407.339.4217
www.xulonpress.com

Paperback ISBN-13: 978-1-6628-3700-5
Ebook ISBN-13: 978-1-6628-3702-9

Acknowledgements

I would like to thank my parents, family, friends, and all of the people who have supported me in following my dreams.

It was the night before St. Patrick's Day, and no one could have prepared Kyndal for the adventure that awaited her. Everything she believed about leprechauns was about to change forever.

Kyndal loved St. Patrick's Day. Her favorite part was getting chocolate gold coins under her pillow that leprechauns only gave to kind little boys and girls.

But, as Kyndal grew older, she stopped believing in leprechauns. Those fairytales were for kids. She had never seen one, so she assumed her parents must have put the coins under her pillow, not the leprechauns.

She tried to stay awake, hoping to catch a glimpse of her parents placing the coins under her pillow, but she soon fell asleep.

Suddenly, she woke in a bed that wasn't hers.

"Where am I?" she said as she looked around the strange bedroom.

On the closet door hung a huge sign that read: *Pick an outfit and get dressed.*

4

There were many beautiful outfits to choose from. She picked a green dress with a glittery shamrock jacket and gold shoes. After she put them on, she looked in the mirror and noticed her ears had become pointed, her eyes had widened, and she was several inches shorter.

"I look like a leprechaun! Cool!" She giggled.

A tall leprechaun lady entered the room.

Kyndal turned to her and said, "Hello, I'm Kyndal. Who are you, and where am I?"

"Welcome to leprechaun headquarters, Kyndal! My name is Mrs. Summers. I'm in charge here. I changed you into a leprechaun because of your kind heart and good deeds. You have been chosen for a special assignment on this special night," Mrs. Summers said.

"L-leprechauns? Leprechauns are real? But why haven't I ever seen one before?" Kyndal asked.

"Of course, we are real!" Mrs. Summers responded with a smile. "We are sneaky because we don't want anyone stealing from us. For centuries, we didn't share our chocolate gold coins with anyone because we feared losing our magic. Then one day, a child who believed showed kindness toward us. In return, we decided to share our coins. That's when we realized that kindness and belief made our magic stronger. Now, every year on the night before St. Patrick's Day, we share our chocolate gold coins with children who have shown kindness towards others."

"I need your help delivering coins to three deserving kids and placing the coins under their pillows. But be careful, these kids may have traps in their bedrooms to try to catch you," Mrs. Summers warned.

"Why would they want to do that?" Kyndal asked.

"Many kids set traps to prove that we are real. So be careful and use your time wisely. You must complete the assignment and return before sunrise. If you're late, the chocolate coins will disappear, and children may stop believing in leprechauns. When they stop believing, our magic and the spirit of St. Patrick Day starts to fade. We can't let this happen. Are you ready, Kyndal?" Mrs. Summers asked.

"Yes!" Kyndal said. "But how do I get to these children?"

Mrs. Summers smiled and said, "Follow me."

They entered a room filled with busy leprechauns preparing chocolate coins while singing, "Sharing kindness is what we do. It makes us happy through and through."

Kyndal and Mrs. Summers danced and sang along as they crossed the room.

HAPPY
ST. PATRICK'S
✤ DAY ✤

HAPPY
ST. PATRICK'S
DAY

Mrs. Summers stopped before a magic door. "This door will take you to the human world where you will deliver the coins. But, before you go, you'll need this," Mrs. Summers added.

She handed Kyndal a map to locate the children, and then Mrs. Summers sprinkled her with magic dust. Instantly, Kyndal rose into the air and began to fly like a bird, leaving a trail of green and gold glitter behind her.

"Remember, you have to deliver all of the coins and return before sunrise," Mrs. Summers warned.

"You can count on me!" Kyndal replied excitedly.

Then, in the blink of an eye, Mrs. Summers was gone!

Kyndal opened the magic door and flew into action.

13

The first child on her list was Max. He had donated two hundred cans of soup to the homeless shelter and helped serve food at the food pantry.

"It's truly kind to donate and serve others," Kyndal said.

As soon as Kyndal flew inside Max's bedroom window, something yanked her upwards and held her against the ceiling. Kyndal struggled for a moment before she realized that Max had attached a magnet to the ceiling. Her jacket, which was made of metallic glitter, got stuck to the magnet and trapped Kyndal.

"Clever boy," Kyndal said. "But not clever enough."
 Kyndal wiggled out of her jacket and floated down to the floor.
 She placed the coins under Max's pillow and flew away quickly,
forgetting her jacket.

Next on Kyndal's list was Rylee. She had helped her elderly neighbor with yard work without being asked.

"That was very thoughtful of her," Kyndal said.

Rylee's bedroom was too dark for Kyndal to see anything. She used her leprechaun magic to switch her glasses to night-vision mode so she could see better.

There were Legos everywhere! She flew over to Rylee's bed, dodging Lego towers as she went. Green and gold glitter swirled behind her and lit up the room like a nightlight.

Kyndal placed the coins under Rylee's pillow. Just as she was about to fly away, Rylee rolled over and hugged Kyndal like a teddy bear. Kyndal remained still, afraid to wake Rylee.

Thankfully, Rylee loosened her grip.

Kyndal slipped out of her arms and flew out of the room as fast as she could.

"Phew! That was too close!" she said.

The last kid on her list was Milana. She had donated all of her savings to the local children's hospital.

"Wow! It was kind of her to give to other kids in need," Kyndal said.

Kyndal scanned Milana's room but didn't spot any traps.

She flew over to Milana's bed and reached out to place the coins
under her pillow when a cage fell over her.
Milana woke up, and Kyndal's cover was blown.

"I knew leprechauns were real!" Milana shouted.

"Yes, we are." Kyndal smiled as she lifted the cage with her magic.

"I'm sorry for the trap," Milana said with a warm smile. "But I just had to see a leprechaun myself. No one else believed me."

"Can I ask you something?" Kyndal gave Milana a curious look. "Why did you donate to the children's hospital?"

"I wanted to help people," replied Milana. "It makes me feel good to do nice things for others."

Kyndal remembered the leprechauns' chant: "Sharing kindness is what we do. It makes us happy through and through."

Filled with joy, she wanted to help Milana. "Would you like to take a selfie with me?" Kyndal asked. "Maybe then the other kids will believe you and know leprechauns are real. And if more kids believe in leprechauns, their magic will be safe!"

"That would be great!" Milana smiled and grabbed her camera off her desk.

Kyndal gave Milana the last of her gold coins, and they took a cool selfie together.

"Thank you!" Milana grinned. "I can't wait to show the other kids at school!"

Kyndal gave Milana a big hug and whispered, "You're welcome. Now keep being kind and don't trap any more leprechauns."

"I promise," Milana giggled.

Kyndal flew away, leaving a trail of green and gold glitter behind her.

She hurried as fast as she could to make it back to headquarters before sunrise. Mrs. Summers beamed when Kyndal flew into sight just before dawn.

Kyndal told Mrs. Summers all about her incredible adventure.

"Their good deeds make me want to share kindness, too!" Kyndal exclaimed. "I learned that doing good for others not only makes them feel good, but it makes me feel good, too!"

Mrs. Summers smiled and said, "You have made it back in perfect time, and it sounds like you have learned something too. I'm very proud of you. I knew I chose the right person when I brought you here. Now, come along. You've had a long night. It's time to get some rest."

She led Kyndal back to the room where she had awakened.
Kyndal was tired from her adventure. She crawled back into the strange bed and soon fell asleep.

She woke up later that morning, back in her bedroom, to the delicious smell of chocolate. Under her pillow was a pile of chocolate coins. "Jackpot! What an amazing dream," she said with excitement.

On the floor, there was a trail of green and gold glitter leading to her closet.

"No way... it couldn't have been real!" she exclaimed.

She dashed to the closet and saw a glittery shamrock jacket, just like the one from her dream.

In the jacket's pocket was a note that read:

*Sharing kindness is what we do. It makes
us happy through and through.
Thanks to you, even more children believe
in us, and our magic is stronger than ever.
Here is the jacket you left.
Keep showing kindness.
I'll see you next year.
– Mrs. S.*

Kyndal smiled. "Sharing kindness is what I do. It makes me happy through and through! This is the best St. Patrick's Day ever!"

Filled with excitement, she hurried off to school in her new pretty jacket, ready to share kindness and celebrate her favorite holiday.

Love each other with genuine affection,
and take delight in honoring each other.
Romans 12:10 (NLT)